CAUGHT UP IN LUST AND BETRAYAL

Dr. Shauntel Peak-Jimenez, Ph.D

© 2021 Dr. Shauntel Peak-Jimenez. All rights reserved. No part of this book may be reproduced or transmitted in any form whatsoever.

Disclaimer: In no way does this book guarantee or promise any specific outcomes. This book is intended for reading entertainment and inspiration. This book is a work of fiction. Names, characters, business, events, and situations are fictitious. Any similarity to actual persons or events is purely coincidental. This book was created for adult readers.

ISBN: 9798760491282

Thank You

Thank you to everyone who believes in me and supports me. I appreciate you more than words can express. To my family and friends, you are amazing, and I love you. Also, thank you to my loved ones who have passed away. Your light still shines bright. Mama, thank you for always encouraging me to write. You are no longer here on earth, but your inspiration continues to guide me.

To anyone who is reading this, never give up on your dreams. Whatever God puts on your heart to do, do it. Believe in yourself and trust that with God, "All Things Are Possible."

Contents

Introduction

It didn't take me long to realize that what felt good to me wasn't good for me. I am so mad at myself for not having the strength to resist temptation. I have allowed myself to be in this situation that is ripping me apart and has ripped my family apart. I am an embarrassment to myself and to my family, and I am sure God isn't pleased with my disgusting behavior either. My mama said she named me "Mya" because that was a beautiful name to her, and I was a beautiful gift from God. But at this point in my life, I don't feel like a beautiful gift, I feel like a curse.

I do feel like I am somewhat beautiful, I mean we all should think positive about ourselves, right? I get a lot of compliments on my features, and I was graciously blessed with curves in all the right places. I love fabulous hairstyles, and a face that is glamorous. But no matter how beautiful other people think I am, my current actions are ugly. See, beauty isn't all about what we see, it's more about what we don't see, a person's attitude, their character, and how they love and appreciate others, which I have been terrible at.

You would think at my age of 40 my life wouldn't be such a mess, but it is. And I am not some messy, drama-filled, "ghetto girl." I am the business owner of a successful marketing firm, a wife, a mother, and very active in my community. But now that I think about it, what are the characteristics of a "ghetto girl?" Maybe that describes me too. When I was a young girl, I always wanted to be the "down chick", but it never felt right to me. But looking at my life today I realize I am no different than some of the young girls and women I never wanted to be like. At least a woman who is really "down" keeps it real. She doesn't lie and hide secrets like I am doing.

I really had a great life, one that many women dream of having. My husband Marquell is a doctor that owns his own medical practice. He is the kind of man I prayed for as a young woman. He is kind, humble, loving, God-fearing, and ambitious just like my Daddy. And he is easy on the eyes too. I have always been attracted to his hazel brown eyes and athletic build. We have two amazing daughters Lyric and London, a beautiful home, and what seemed to be a perfect marriage until Quan (short for Quandray) showed back up in my life. That is a day I will regret for-ever.

I should have learned my lesson from dealing with Quan years ago. When I was younger, we met at a club, hit it off right away, and became inseparable. We were together for three years. We had a great relationship until he decided he wanted to be unfaithful. He was a low-down cheating dog then but somehow with his slick taking self and manipulating ways he convinced me he was a changed man. And you would think after all these years he would be. But responding to his message to me on social media was the biggest mistake I ever made. As the saying goes, all that glitters isn't gold. And the grass isn't always greener on the other side either. There's a lot of mud and weeds mixed in with that grass too. I should have known that because like I said Quan had already cheated on me back in the day.

He cheated with my cousin Kesha. She reluctantly told me that after a night of them being out at the same club together he offered to drive her home and things went too far. I was devastated, but like an idiot, I stayed with him. I forgave Kesha too, but I will never trust her like that again. Then not long after that Quan cheated with the mother of his child. He already had a daughter when we met. I left him alone after that and didn't look back, well not until recently. I told myself I was done with Quan and was leaving him alone for good. And I should have kept that promise to myself. Now, have a deeper look into my chaotic life and you will understand why I am in the situation I am in.

CHAPTER 1

The Beginning-The Emotional Affair

My husband Marquell has been kind of different since his sister was murdered by her estranged husband 6 months ago. He talked to her often about leaving her husband for good, but she never stayed gone until one day it was too late. Marquell was supposed to meet with her the night she was murdered and take her to dinner, but he had a meeting that ran over so before he could get there, he received a call from his mother telling him that Daphne had been murdered. He always tells me he is ok but deep inside I know he feels guilty about his meeting running over and him not getting there in time. And that has affected his communication with me.

Even through all of that, we have managed to still stay close as ever. He is the light of my life and I love him dearly. I call him the "light of my life" because he has a special way of brightening up my day. I am always there for him showing him affection and love in any way I can. We have been married for 10 wonderful years and he is the man of my dreams. He adores me and will do anything for me. Both of us have devoted so many years to our careers so we decided beginning next year we will cut back on our work hours and just enjoy each other more. With Daphne being murdered I think it has made Marquell look at life differently and want to enjoy it more and that's fine with me. I love spending time with him, and I love the life and family we have built. I can't imagine anything ever breaking our bond.

Quan has contacted me through social media, and we have connected. He still looks good too. He looks the same as he did years ago except he has dreads now. I don't care how good he looks I am not going backward in my life. I am not attracted to him romantically. I only connected with him through social media so he can see the pictures I post of my fine-fine husband and beautiful family. I know that sounds petty, but it feels good showing Quan that I made it without him, something he said would never happen. I am surprised he reached out to me it has been so long since we have seen each other. I thought long and hard about reconnecting with him but it's only social media so it can't hurt, right?

It has been a few months since we have reconnected, and he has been very respectful toward me and my marriage. He may comment on a picture here and there, but nothing more than that. So, I am surprised he has started sending me private messages. I don't think I should respond because I know Marquell won't like that at all. He is aware Quan and I dated back in the day, but he knows he has nothing to worry about. So maybe he won't be bothered after all. But if there is nothing to it, why am I trying to hide? I know this is pathetic but even with all the attention my husband gives me I still crave more, and honestly, I feel flattered that Quan is stepping up the attention he has been showing me. I don't know why I feel flattered I just do. Maybe something inside of me needs to be fixed because it makes no sense to have an amazing, kind, loving, and successful husband at home but here I am entertaining this foolishness on the side.

The communication between Quan and I has been getting more frequent over the past few weeks, and we have even taken trips down "memory lane." My sister Ebony said that Quan and I are having an emotional affair, but I don't see it that way. I am just being a supportive friend to him, and he is being a supportive friend to me.

She doesn't know what she is talking about. I shouldn't have even told Ebony what was going on because she doesn't even really get on social media, so she doesn't understand how it works. She said I have been talking about Quan way too much and that what Quan and I are doing is inappropriate. She acts like we are sleeping together or something. I would never let things go that far. I am so mad at her right now because she told Grandma Veronica ("Ronnie") I have been communicating with Quan. My grandma sat me down and expressed her concern to me and I get what she is saying. But it's not what they think it is.

It's been months now since Quan and I have been communicating privately through social media today he asked me for my phone number. I said "no" at first, but I quickly changed my mind and said "yes" I really want to hear his voice. I told him he can only call me during certain hours, and this is not going to be an ongoing thing and he agreed. He just sent me a private message to let me know exactly what time he will be calling today. It is getting close to that time, and I am nervously awaiting his call. I have no idea why I am nervous but I am. The phone is ringing, I need to take a deep breath before I answer it so I can feel more relaxed. I finally get the courage to answer it and hearing Quan's voice feels so good.

I can't believe we stayed on the phone talking, laughing, and sharing memories for over an hour. I can tell by the way he was talking that he is a changed man, and I am so proud of him for that. He told me he was sorry for how he treated me in the past and he thanked me for being his friend today.

He told me what seems like a million times that Marquellis lucky to have me. And that made me smile. On the drive from my office to my house I had all these thoughts running through my head about Quan. Thoughts that made me feel guilty. Hearing his voice did something to me. He seems like a better communicator than Marquell right now. I know Marquell is going through something, but I still need his emotional support, but he is lacking that right now. We talk but he shuts down emotionally and he is not as open with me as he used to be. I know it's just a part of the grieving process he is going through, but does that mean my emotional needs should be neglected? Now that I am thinking about it, I realize I should be talking to Marquell about our issues and not Quan. But having Quan as a friend isn't a bad thing.

I am glad I beat Marquell home because I felt like I had guilt all over my face. And I needed some time alone to take a hot bath, light some candles, and reflect on my behavior. I thought Quan was out of my system, but I am realizing he is not. To be honest, I have wondered about him from time to time and even thought I would enjoy hearing from him again, but God kept him out of my life for a reason.

CHAPTER 2

Shattered Vows

When the text messages and phone calls were getting out of hand everything in me said "stop," but I kept going, and I am ashamed to say that what I thought was innocent with Quan has now turned into a full-blown extra marital affair. Our messages and phone calls led to several in person meetings and that has escalated to his bedroom, the living room, the car, and wherever else we want to get intimate. And all this sneaking and creeping is getting to me. I have no idea how I am balancing it all, two men, two children, and a career. It helps a lot that Quan knows he is my "side dude" so he accepts that and doesn't cause me any problems. He knows his role and he plays it well. He also does his thing with whoever and I still have my family. We agreed no attachment would happen. But feelings are getting deeper between us and this whole thing is starting to feel more complicated by the minute.

Marquell has no clue about what is going on, and there are times I feel sorry for him. He doesn't deserve this type of treatment and if he ever finds out about my affair, he will leave me. And that is not something I am ready to deal with. I don't know how I became stuck in between two men. Well, yes, I know. I just can't believe I allowed this to happen. I have always taken my vows seriously and I never imagined cheating on my husband. My eyes are drawn to my wedding ring, I don't know why I am staring at it with tears running down my face, that isn't going to change anything. My wedding ring has always been something special and significant to me, now it just seems like a piece of metal. My actions have me feeling different about my marriage.

I can't believe I crawl in the bed with Marquell every night as if nothing is going on. There was one time we were intimate, and I almost called him Quan, I caught myself before it came out. I don't know what would have happened if that would have slipped, but I know the outcome wouldn't have been good.

Being with Quan is so different than being with Marquell. Quan is adventurous, he is a risk-taker, he dresses fly, and he is a "bad boy" in many people's eyes. He had a couple of incidents with the law when he was a young "hot head," but he has stayed out of trouble ever since. He works as a construction worker, loves his motorcycle, his old school cars, and his boat. He just loves living life. He has a dope swag that is mesmerizing. Being with him makes me feel energized and youthful. And I love how he says "Mya." It's something about how my name rolls off his tongue that turns me on. I don't know if I am "catching feelings" for Quan because it is something new or if I am really falling in love with him. All I know is being with him feels good. But how can something that feels so good be so bad?

I was so focused on my thoughts about Quan I don't even realize Marquellis asking me a question. I finally become aware of his question and respond, then he asks me several times if I am ok. Part of me feels like he is starting to realize something is "off." I have been sneaking off to answer phone calls or check my text messages, preoccupied with thoughts of Quan, I never leave my phone unattended, I have been conveniently working later and later, not answering his calls when I am with Quan, not hanging out with Marquell and the girls like I used to, and I haven't been into Marquell intimately. Marquell is a smart man, so I know he knows something is up and if he doesn't it won't take long for him to figure it out. But if I continue to be careful my secret should be safe. I don't want to lose my family. Honestly, I want Marquell and Quan. I guess you can say "I want my cake and eat it too." I feel like I have the best of both worlds. I can't believe I have this twisted way of thinking. I don't even feel like myself anymore. This affair has turned me into someone I don't even recognize.

It's weird because I am here with Marquell physically, but my heart is with Quan. When I am not with Quan, I wonder what he is doing or who he is doing. The thought of Quan being with another woman bothers me. That's how I know I am in too deep. Every chance I get I am trying to be with Quan. Since Marquell works late hours at times, that has been easy to do. I make up a reason to take the girls to my parent's house or Grandma "Ronnie's" house and I am escaping to the arms of Quan.

Quan's touch is like poetry on my skin. He makes every inch of my body crave for more. He makes my body tingle from the top of my head to my bottom of my feet. He knows every inch of my body and how to please me in every way. And he "rocks my boat" if you know what I mean. But why do I feel like I have been thrown out of the boat and I am drowning? What kind of stronghold does this man have on me? What spell has he put on me that has me willing to give up everything for him, if I am ever caught? But I can't stop seeing him even if I wanted to.

Fast forward. As of today, my affair with Quan has been going on for almost a year. I know I am ridiculous. I can hardly look at myself in the mirror at times. I admit I have never been on drugs, but I am addicted to Quan.

CHAPTER 3

Exposed

I had a great day today and secured a contract with a high-end client. I was excited to share my news with both Marquell and Quan and both are so happy for me. When I got home today Marquell and the girls had a cake for me and we had a wonderful celebration. Quan has also asked me to go to dinner tonight. I haven't been out with him in public and I am skeptical about that. But after some light begging, I agreed to go to a restaurant far away from where we live. So, we chose a nice restaurant in a nice, secluded area an hour away. Now I just must find a convincing lie to get out of the house. Our little family celebration is over so I will just tell Marquell I am going out with a few people from the office to celebrate. He has to get up very early in the morning, so I know he won't ask to go with me. And that worked like a charm. As I am getting ready everything feels wrong and right at the same time.

I decided not to drive to the restaurant myself but to ride with Quan. I will just hide my car in his garage as usual. The drive to the restaurant was interesting and I wasn't expecting Quan to open up to me about his feelings about us. I almost choked on my drink when he said, "he wants me to leave Marquell and be with him." Part of me wanted to say "yes" but the bigger part of me said "no." I am so confused about him thinking I would actually leave my family. I just can't hurt them like that. What I am doing is bad enough. I love Quan and he said, "he loves me," but being together in an exclusive relationship is just not possible. I know I should just end things right now but my feelings for him are deeper than I can explain with words.

Dinner was great and I am having the time of my life. We finished eating over an hour ago and we have just been sitting here enjoying each other's company. I know I must get back home soon. But Quan just asked me to go to a Jazz Club a few minutes from here. Quan goes there frequently and said "it's cool and not very busy through the week. So, there won't be a lot of people there." He knows I am worried about that. I don't want this affair broadcast in public. It's very hard for me to resist Quan so I agreed to go. I am going to text Marquell to let him know I will be home a little late, so he won't be worried. I know he is probably sleeping by now but at least when he sees my text, he will feel like I am being respectful by letting him know.

We just arrived at the Jazz Club and it's beautiful in here and relaxing. The vibe is good, and the staff is friendly. This is the perfect way to end our perfect evening. And it feels good to be with Quan in this type of environment, no hiding, just having a good time. We have our table tucked away in the back of the club, under the dim light and the ambiance is amazing. No worries at all. Well, that was not until I hear someone call my name. "Mya is that you?" I heard in a confused-sounding voice. I looked up trying to keep my expression normal like I am not doing anything wrong. "Hey Chris," I said. I think to myself, oh Lord, I am caught. Chris is Marquell's friend. What in the world is he doing here? I find out his cousin moved out this way and they decided to visit the Jazz Club tonight. Out of all the seats we could have chosen we sat close to the bathroom and as Chris was walking to the bathroom, he noticed me. I can't believe this is happening. I always heard "What's done in the dark always comes to the light" and I see right now that is very true.

Chris gave me a hug and looked at Quan with one eyebrow raised and asked, "and who are you?" I thought to myself take your nosey self back to your table. Before Quan could respond I blurted out "he works for me at the office." Chris said "oh, ok." But I knew that didn't make sense. Why am I out late at night an hour away from home in a romantic environment with this man that works for me? I know Chris and he is definitely tellingMarquell. And I was right, Marquell and I just woke up the next morning, and as we are laying in the bed talking, Marquell says "hmmm… that's odd. Chris called me late last night. He usually doesn't call me. He usually sends me a text message. I hope everything is ok." I have got to think quick, so I am rubbing Marquell on his back and before I know it, we are getting intimate. I am buying some time and trying to come up with something quick because I know what Chris is about to tell Marquell.

I can't even come up with a good lie before I hear Marquell say "Now Chris is texting me. He told me to call him right away." Marquell is calling Chris right now. My heart is beating so hard I feel like it is about to jump out of my chest, my palms are sweating, and I need to go to the bathroom. I have to step out of the room and go downstairs to get my thoughts together. I barely make it out of the room good and I hear Marquell yelling my name. And I can tell by his tone he is very upset. I am on my way back into the bedroom to speak with him now.

With fury in his eyes, he asks me "Where did you go last night and who were you with?" He looks away for a second then looks right back at me and said, "and you better not lie to me!" My body feels like I can't move. I am numb and scared. Do I tell the truth or lie? Of course, I am going to lie that's what I do. I act shocked and say "Huh? I sent you a text message saying I was going to be coming home late." I rolled my eyes and shook my head as if in disbelief and ask, "what did Chris tell you?"Whatever he thinks he saw he didn't? Some of the people I work with went to a Jazz Club after we ate dinner. Most of them left early except for a few of us. Two of the other ladies that work for me were in the bathroom when Chris came to the table, so he assumed it was just me and the guy there alone. Instead of him being a man and asking he came to his own conclusion about what was going on. If Chris would have asked, we both would have told him that the other ladies went to the bathroom." As I look at Marquell's face I can tell he believes me. So, I keep making Chris look like the bad guy. I affectionally grab Marquell's hand, look him in his eyes and say "Chris is being messy. Baby, he has hidden jealousy toward our marriage because he didn't work out." The more I talk the more convincing I sound. To my surprise, Marquell looks at me, smiles, apologizes, and gives me a big hug. I am glad he can't see my face because I am smirking because Chris didn't win. Marquell didn't believe a word Chris said, or did he?

CHAPTER 4

What's Done in the Dark Will Eventually Come to Light

I haven't seen Quan in over a month, and he understands. Since the situation happened with Chris, I had to start laying low. I have been the perfect loving and attentive wife, and extra careful not to do anything that is a red flag to Marquell. He already told me "I have been dressing differently and wearing more makeup." I told him that is because I am trying new things out, and he said, "he likes it." Marquell knows I like to look good and feel good.

Even though I haven't seen Quan in person for a while we have still been texting one another and talking on the phone, but we miss each other so much, so tonight we are hooking up for a movie and dinner. We will be at his house; I am not that crazy to go out in public with him again. I was lucky to lie my way out of that situation with Chris, so I am not even going down that road again.

I tell Marquell "I am going to Ebony's house tonight." "Are you taking the girls with you?" he asks. "No" I replied. We are having a girl's night." "That's cool," he says as he kisses me on my forehead. As I am pulling out of our driveway, I feel bad all over again. I found a way out of the affair, and I should have just left Quan alone and focused on my marriage and my family. But here I am again falling to temptation that I know I should be resisting.

Things have been wonderful between Marquell and I the last month, and I know that is because I wasn't sleeping with Quan. I had the space to focus on Marquell and our marriage. But sometimes he still seems a little distant emotionally, but I can tell he is working on things. We had a serious talk and I told him "I want him to let his emotions out, communicate better, and work on healing from Daphne's death." And I am so proud of him for the progress he is making. He joined an online prayer and support group, and it is helping him a lot.

The more I am thinking about Marquell and the amazing man he is I feel the urge to turn around and go back home and just hold him and my girls. My family means a lot to me, and this web of deceit must end. Even though I am a mess I feel God tugging on my heart. I feel the conviction. I feel the "warning before destruction." Matter of fact I feel a change of heart happening.

I know Marquell has been praying for our marriage and tonight I feel his prayers hitting my soul. I need to pull over for a second so I can think. Do I keep driving toward Quan's house or do I turn around and go back home? Five minutes have passed by, and I am still sitting in the same spot on the side of the road, still in the same position of not knowing what to do. Well, I know what I should do but I don't know how to do it. And who can I talk to? I can't share with anyone that I am having an affair.

I hear my text message alert and I just know it's Quan, but it's not, it's Marquell. He just sent me the sweetest message. That should be my sign to turn around and go back home, right? But I just want to see Quan one more time and then I am ending things with him. Matter of fact that's what I am going to tell him when I get to his house. This drive is so different I feel worse than I ever have. For the first time, I am feeling very remorseful and ashamed of myself.

I parkin Quan's garage and get out of the car. He greets me with a tight hug. And he looks so good and smells so good. I sit down at the kitchen table where he has a beautiful setting. He cooked for me, has soft music playing, and everything is so romantic. I want to tell him I can't see him anymore, but the words just won't come out. And before I know it, I find myself cuddled on the couch with him, watching a movie. All the feelings that I thought died on my way over here are alive and stronger than ever. He looks at me and says, "I missed you, baby." "I missed you too" I responded. That has led to a passionate kiss and here we are again tangled up in the sheets once again.

After being here for a few hours I decide to shower, leave, and go home. But I at least need to show up at Ebony's house for a few minutes, in case Marquell asks her "if I came over tonight?" I don't think he will. But I am covering all bases. Because I know she won't lie to him if he asks. I made it to Ebony's house, and we are having a good conversation about life. She is my little sister but wise in so many ways. She asks me "If I have been sleeping because I looked drained." I told her "I just have a lot going on" and left it at that.

I have been here for an hour and need to get back home. So, I am leaving. Walking back in the house feels so different than when I left. I don't feel so happy and excited. Possible consequences of my behavior are starting to set in, and I feel like something bad is going to happen.

Fast forward. Things have taken a turn for the worse. I have continued to see Quan ever since the night I felt like I should turn around and go home. It's been weeks since that night, and we are back at it. And it's affecting my relationship with my husband once again. Part of me wants all of this to end but I can't end it and Quan won't end it. But how long can this go on? Not forever. Something must change. And little do I know; things are about to change, and not in a good way.

I just received a text message from Marquell saying, "we need to talk so come right home when you leave the office." "OK," I reply. I send another message asking him "Is everything ok?" He replied, "we just need to talk." I have no clue what he wants to talk about, but I hope it is good. I have a meeting shortly and I won't be home for a couple of hours. Then I will figure out what all this is about.

That seemed like the longest two hours ever, but I am finally on my way home. Pulling up to our house, I see that Marquell is already home. I grab my things out of the car and head toward the front door, but before I can put my key in the lock Marquell opens the door. I walk in the house, but he doesn't greet me with a hug as he usually does. So, I try to kiss him, but he pulls away. "What's wrong?" I ask. "Did something bad happen at the office?" "No," he says. "But something bad is happening in my marriage." I feel a lump in my throat, and I can feel myself begin to "shaking like a leaf." And at the same time, Marquell starts crying hysterically, pounding his fist on our dining room table to the point where the vase falls off and breaks. He knows something but to what extent I am not sure. Now, things are so quiet in here you can hear a "pin drop." It feels eerie and not like our home at all.

As I am looking at Marquell, he looks angrier than he has ever looked in all our years together. Now he is hitting the wall and he just put a hole in it. "Stop Marquell, you are going to scare the girls! If you were going to act like this, why did you have my parents drop them off?" If looks could kill I would be dead right now because the way he just looked at me is scaring me. And he didn't reply to what I said. "What's going on?" I ask him. He grabs my wrist tight and says, "you tell me!" I need to sit down. Because this is not good. I think he knows something about Quan. It seems like hours have gone by, but it has only been a few minutes, Marquell has left the room and I am still sitting here trying to figure out what is happening.

I hear footsteps coming near me. Marquell is standing over me, clenching his fists and says, "How long have you been sleeping with Quan?" Oh my God! How does he know? What does he know? Does he have his gun on him? Is he going to shoot me? They always say, "watch out for the quiet ones," but as I see him sit next to me at the table, lay his head on the table, and start crying again I realize he is just hurting. "Please tell me the truth Mya. I deserve that" he says. I say, "I am not sleeping with Quan." I can't admit to that. But Marquell looks at me and says, "You are a liar." Then he shows me pictures of Quan and I, a print-out of my social media messages, phone records, proof of my text messages, and he put a "tracking device" on my car. The nerve of him I thought. But no, it's the nerve of me. Marquell says "he saw too many signs and had a feeling I was cheating on him, and since I didn't want to be honest and tell him what has been going on. He hired a private investigator."

Marquell and I have been talking for almost five hours and I told him everything. I can't deny the affair when the proof is right here in front of us both. The hurt in his eyes is devastating to me. How could I let this happen? He just asked me if I love Quan. With tears running down my face, "Yes, I do. And I love you too." I reply. I don't want to lie anymore, I am tired. Of course, Marquell thinks I am stupid for messing up my marriage for someone who cheated on me and treated me like dirt. But Quan is a changed man. "Are you leaving me Marquell?" I ask. "No, I am not." I let out a sigh of relief, but then he says, "You are leaving." "Marquell, don't do this to the girls!" I beg. He looks me up and down with a look of disgust and says "no, you did this to the girls!"

CHAPTER 5

The Decision

It's been 6 weeks since Marquell kicked me out of the house. I have been staying at a hotel near my office. Even though I am not living with Marquell and the girls right now I have been to the house several times to visit the girls. They are so confused about what is going on, but I am glad they are old enough to understand that sometimes parents have disagreements and need a little time apart.

Marquell said, "he doesn't want a divorce right now; he just needs time away from me." That's understandable. Right now, he isn't even speaking to me unless it has something to do with the girls. As far as Quan, I talked to him a few times on the phone, but I haven't seen him. He acts like he feels sorry for me since Marquell found out about us. But I think in a way he is happy about it. Because he said, "now he can have me to himself."

I am so tired of living in this hotel, but Marquell and I agreed not to tell his family or my family about what is going on, so I can't stay with anyone we know. I am living a lie like everything is fine at home when it is not. And Marquell said, "Since I am good at lying and pretending no one will even think we are having problems" and he is right. My parents would be so disappointed if they knew about my actions. Not to mention my dad and Bear can't stand Quan. They didn't like him back in the day and their feelings haven't changed about him.

I have been considering asking Quan if I can move in with him until all of this blows over. Marquell isn't speaking to me anyway, he won't know and probably won't even care. I just need to get out of this hotel, it is so depressing. I spend as much time as I can at the office but then I come back here to this hotel. It's a very nice hotel, but it's lonely here and I thought by now I would be back home, but that hasn't happened, and I don't know if it ever will. I have never seen Marquell so mad at me. I really think it's over and that he is just trying to get comfortable with getting a divorce. I know he said, "he doesn't want a divorce," but I feel like he really does. He says one thing but acts differently.

Two days later I have gone against my better judgment and asked Quan "if I can stay with him" he agreed to let me stay at his house for as long as I need to. So, I am on my way to the house to get some more of my things. I will be staying with Quan until Marquell lets me come back home. As I walk in the house Marquell doesn't say a word to me. He doesn't even look my way. The girls are happy to see me. That makes me smile and feel loved. I hope Marquell says something to me, but he doesn't so I am just going to take my things and leave. He is not the only one that can have an attitude. If he doesn't want to say anything to me then I won't say anything to him.

I have been staying with Quan for about three months now and the word has gotten out that he and I are living together. It feels like everyone knows. We do a lot of things together outside of the house and have not tried to hide the fact that we live together. It is what it is. Marquell doesn't want me, so I moved on. My friends and family are upset with me. But now I realize everything happens for a reason, and with Quan is where I want to be. I feel like things worked out exactly how they were meant to. I miss Lyric and London and I wish I could see them more, but Marquell is not allowing that to happen. I asked Marquell if I could get the girls a couple times a week and on the weekends. He said, "there is no way the girls are coming to stay with Quan and I." So, for now, I spend a few hours with them every week at my parent's house. But Marquell can't keep my girls away from me forever. I am happy living with

Quan, but I would be happier if my girls were here with me. But I can't do anything about that right now. Marquell is just being a jerk. All this has nothing to do with the girls.

The longer I live with Quan the less guilty I feel about everything. I deserve to be happy too. Quan makes me feel so good and he is good to me. And I sacrificed everything for him. But honestly, there are times I feel like I am not completely over Marquell and I miss what we had. I wish he didn't hate me so much so we could at least be friends.

Today Marquell let me know that he is filing for divorce. That makes me kind of sad because I never planned on any of this happening. I never planned on choosing Quan over Marquell. Marquell made that choice for me. He is the one that kicked me out of the house, and he stopped dealing with me, it wasn't the other way around. I tried to fight for my family. I asked Marquell "if we could go to a marriage counselor," and I tried to make my wrongs right, but nothing worked. So, I have moved on with my life. I am not proud of how things have turned out. But I had to pick up the pieces and continue to live. I accepted the fact a long time ago that things are over between Marquell and I. And when he divorces me, I will be totally free of guilt and judgment from others. Well, I hope so.

I have never filed for divorce because that would have definitely made me look like the bad guy. Like I divorced

Marquell to be with Quan and that wouldn't have been true. But I know divorce is a hard decision for Marquell because he always said, "he wanted his children to grow up in a two-parent household because he didn't have that opportunity." It would be much easier to feel better about the divorce if Marquell was a horrible man, but he isn't. Matter of fact he is a wonderful man. I just got caught up.

The decision to move in with Quan has been absolutely amazing so far. It was awkward at first but with each day that passes, I feel more comfortable. But I didn't think about how my decision would affect everyone else or my relationship with others. Even some of my employees have been looking at me with a side-eye. Especially the day Quan brought me flowers and lunch to the office. Many people seemed very uncomfortable with that. I mean everything is out in the open, so I didn't understand why they were so bothered. But after I thought about it, I understood that didn't look good because even though Marquell and I have been separated for a while, technically we are still married. And after all, Quan is the man, I was having an affair with. Or is that currently having an affair with since I am still married?

After all, I have sacrificed, I hope things work out with Quan. I hope it was all worth it. I hope I don't end up regretting any decisions I have made to be with him. Because now my marriage is past saving. Moving in with Quan was another knife in the back to Marquell. He always had my back and I stabbed him in his with my lies, secrets, and betrayal. But I can't change anything, what's done is done. Now I can only learn from my mistakes and make my relationship with Quan work. But can things get any messier? Yes, they can, and they will.

CHAPTER 6

The Altercation

I just got off the phone with Mama and she let me know the girls are staying all night with them. I am going to stop by to see them on our way to dinner. Yes, that means Quan is with me. But it's ok. I will have him park across the street where Daddy can't see him. Mama won't say too much about Quan being in front of their house, but Daddy will have a fit, and plus Bear is over there too, so I don't want any problems between my man, my dad, and my brother. I just want to see my girls, give them a hug and kiss, and be on my way.

As we pull up to the house, I tell Quan to" turn the music down." My parents live in a nice, quiet neighborhood and nobody wants to hear all that "racket" as my dad says. I lean over and give Quan a kiss on the cheek. "Give me five minutes baby. I will be right out." He says "ok" and pulls his cell phone out of his pocket to "pass the time." When he has free time, he loves to look at old school cars on his phone.

As soon I get in the house, I give my parents and Bear a hug. I know they are still not happy with my choices, but they don't mistreat me in any way. And it's always great to see each other. Daddy has the kitchen smelling good as usual. He made what he calls his "famous lasagna" I don't know about it being famous but it sure is delicious. I make my way to the guest bedroom and surprise the girls. After 10 minutes of laughing and talking I need to go because Quan and I have dinner plans. To my amazement, nobody even mentions his name and that is good seeing how he is right outside parked across the street.

After telling everyone "Goodbye" I head toward the door to leave. As I am walking across the street to get back in the car, I see Marquell pulling up to my parents' house. I think to myself why is he here? Mama said, "the girls are here for the night." But Mama wasn't aware Lyric called Marquell to bring her pajamas she forgot to pack in her bag until Lyric told her. My first instinct is to go back in the house before Marquell notices Quan is in the car. I have always managed to avoid seeing Marquell while I am out with Quan in public. But going back in the house means

I have to listen to Marquell's sarcastic remarks toward me, and I am not in the mood for that.

The only thing I can do is get in the car and leave. If Marquell sees Quan I know he will tell Daddy and I will just deal with Daddy fussing later. I go to open the passenger side of the door and I notice Marquell has parked, gotten out of his car, and is looking at me. I think to myself, what is he looking at? And I realize Marquell sees me getting in on the passenger side of the car, so he knows Quan is driving. But Quan is still looking at his phone, so he isn't paying attention to what is going on. At the same time, Quan finally looks up at me, Marquell yells my name. Frozen in place I try to figure out what to do. I decide to answer Marquell in case it has something to do with the girls. "What's up?" I say to Marquell. He calls me over to where he is standing. As I am walking towards him. I look back at Quan and he has an angry expression on his face. Marquell explains to me why he is at my parent's house and asks me "How have you been?" "Fine," I reply. I can't believe he is being nice to me, and we are having a decent conversation. We have been chatting about the girls for a few minutes, and I hear "beep-beep" as Quan blows the horn. I put my finger up to say "wait a minute" but then he begins to blow the horn longer. I don't' know what his problem is, maybe he thinks Marquell is arguing with me about him being there. He did say "he didn't like seeing me with Quan," but then he instantly started talking about the girls.

I guess I have been taking too long because now Quan is getting out of the car, I look toward the car as I hear the car door slam.

I think to myself what is Quan doing? He comes over to where Marquell and I are standing, yelling my name, cussing, and talking crazy to Marquell. He grabs my hand and says, "You okay baby?" "Yes, I replied." All the commotion has gotten the attention of Mama, Daddy, and Bear, and I see them coming outside. "What's going on?" Daddy yells as he walks toward all three of us. Now Marquell and Quan are both yelling at the top of their lungs, and things are escalating. "Let's go, Quan!" I yell as loud as I can, to yell over both him and Marquell. But that doesn't work. So, I am going to grab Quan's arm and lead him toward the car, but before I can Quan looks at Marquell and says "You are just mad because your wife chose a real man. You couldn't make her happy, but I do. I do what you can't do in and out of the bedroom." With a tear in my eye, I look at Quan and say "that's enough! Stop it!" And Marquell has a look of pain on his face that is really breaking my heart. I don't even think he knows what to say. So, he looks at me and says "Wow this is what you wanted? This type of man? Best wishes to you both. I hope you are happy." Our eyes are locked, and I am so hurt for Marquell. But before I can say anything to him, I feel Quan grab my hand and say, "let's go." I am so glad the girls didn't hear anything that just happened. As Quan and I are leaving I see my parents and Bear hugging Marquell. Then as we are getting in the car, I hear my dad call Quan's name. So, Quan turns back around. He says, "I am going to go see what your dad wants." "Okay," I replied. "But I am not going with you. This is too much for me. I feel stressed and I am ready to go. But I am curious about what Daddy wants to talk to Quan about.

I keep my eyes fixed on Quan as he walks up to Daddy. And I feel the urge to get out of the car. So, I do. It's not fair that I am leaving Quan to face my Daddy, this is my mess too. My mama, Bear, and Marquell are still by the door talking. As I am walking toward Daddy and Quan, Marquell looks at me and begins shaking his head, as if to say you are pitiful. As I approach Daddy and Quan, I hear Daddy yell "When you mess with my family you mess with me!" Marquell is family to Daddy. And Daddy punches Quan in the face. Quan puts his hand on his face where Daddy punched him and says, "I know you didn't punch me, old man!" "I did and I will again!" Daddy yells. Marquell, Mama, and Bear rush over here to get Daddy and calm him down. But now Quan is trying to run up on Daddy to fight him! Is Quan crazy? But before he could get to Daddy, Bear gives Quan the business. And Quan ends up on the ground. As Quan is getting off the ground so we can leave Marquell says "Hey man! I guess you should have been focusing on how to fight instead of focusing on sleeping with my wife!" Quan doesn't say a word. We just get in the car and drive off.

CHAPTER 7

The Regret

We didn't make it to dinner, and I am trying to process what happened at my parent's house. I don't know what was more shocking, the incident or Marquell and I communicating like we both have some sense (which we do). Quan made a couple of remarks about doing something to Bear, but I know he is just mad and talking trash. He better never try to do anything to hurt my brother. Quan was in the wrong and he just needs to admit that and move on.

It has now been weeks since the incident happened and Marquell and I are getting along better. Our divorce date is coming up soon and we both are ready to move on. I heard Marquell has a new doctor friend he met at a conference, and he has been spending a lot of time with her. I don't try to be in his business, but his Mama felt the need to share that with me. I think she enjoyed telling me that. I saw her at the grocery store, and she followed me down the aisle just to share that information. I am not jealous or mad at Marquelle and he doesn't have to tell me what is going on in his life. We are not together. He deserves to be happy.

But since we have been communicating better, I am beginning to really miss being with him and the girls. Things are just not the same with Quan. I built a life and a family with Marquell and I really miss that. I miss our family dinners; I miss spending quality time with Marquell and the girls, I miss Marquell's kisses on my forehead, I miss the way he laughs at my corny jokes, I miss the way we used to stay up until 2 a.m. in the morning talking, I miss the way Marquell knew something was wrong with me before I even said a word, I miss the random text messages asking how my day is going, I miss the compliments, I miss the dances in the kitchen to our favorite song, I miss the walks in the park, I even miss the intimate moments we shared. Gosh, I miss him. Right now, I wish I could turn back the hands of time. Now that I am on the outside looking in, I see what I had and how wonderful it was. And I am not feeling this way because I heard Marquell is seeing someone. I have felt this way before I found that out.

I wonder what Marquell will say if I call and ask him if I can come by and see him so we can talk? I guess I will never know if I don't try. So, let me call him. He tells me "We don't need to talk in person, but we can talk on the phone." But I need to talk to him face to face. I want to give him a genuine apology and make sure it's really over before we head to divorce court. I am so confused, and I thought this is the life I wanted but it really isn't. I made a huge mistake moving in with Quan instead of continuing to fight for my marriage and family, and I regret it. I want things to be like they used to be before Quan showed up. I want Marquell to forgive me and I want him to want me back. I want to rekindle what we had. I know that with Marquell it was true love. The way he loved me was like something out of a fairy tale. I chose lust over love and now I am paying for it.

I don't even feel the same when Quan touches me. I want him to touch me less and less. I slept on the couch last night and the night before. I acted like I fell asleep doing some work and just didn't make it to the bed in time. But that's not it. I want Marquell and my family back, and I am not feeling this anymore. The excitement has worn off and reality has set in. I don't want Quan for a husband. I thought I did but I don't. I want MY husband! The little things that once bothered me about Marquell are now the things I miss so much about him.

Sitting in this dark room all alone is giving me peace. I can close my eyes and imagine I am living the life I neglected, the life I chose Quan over, and the life God blessed me with. My grandma Ronnie always says "nothing is too hard for the Lord" but I think she meant everything except healing my marriage. Because how can God fix this mess that I created? I wish he would though because we all make mistakes, he understands that right? If I don't know anything else, I know to go to God for the help I need. With a feeling of disgrace and disappointment in myself I say "Lord, if you give me my family back, I promise to do right." I hope he helps me rebuild what I have allowed to be torn down.

Things have really been going downhill with Quan and I, but he doesn't suspect it has anything to do with how I am feeling about Marquell. He just thinks I am overwhelmed from work and the upcoming court date. I know I should just move out and get my own place but part of me doesn't like being alone. So, I am just going with the flow.

Marquell texted me earlier and said he wants me to come and pick up the rest of my things. I don't have much left there, but I will go to the house this weekend, I have some free time then. I guess this means things are really coming to an end with us. I really don't know how to feel. I mean I knew the day was coming but I didn't expect it to be a sad occasion. I always thought I would be happy and celebrating

It's finally the weekend and I am heading to the house to get the rest of my things. But this time when I get to the door, I have to ring the doorbell because Marquell has taken my house key back. He opens the door and surprisingly gives me a big hug. Don't let go I am thinking to myself. I wish this embrace could last forever. I begin to gather my things and hear Marquell coming in the room. I ask him "Is this what you really want?" He replied, "I didn't but you left me with no choice." "Marquell, I am sorry. Can you please forgive me? I never stopped loving you and I want my family back." He looks at me stunned and says, "You what? You can't be serious." "Baby, I am serious" I reply. "Will you give me another chance?" "I can't. You hurt me too bad, and the girls. And I don't trust you," he says. Hearing those words make me feel hurt and sad. But I understand where he is coming from. "Are you seeing someone?" I ask him. "No' he responds. "I have a friend but that's all she is. I won't touch another woman intimately until our divorce is final." I feel relieved to hear that. And I should have already known that because that's just the kind man Marquell is.

41

As I am walking out of the house to leave, I feel Marquell put one hand on each of my shoulders, then he bends over and whispers in my ear "And for the record, I will always love you." I turn around and we embrace once again but this time our embrace is followed by a deep passionate kiss. I hope this kiss leads to something else, but it doesn't. So, I am headed back home.

CHAPTER 8

"You Reap What You Sow"

Even though Marquell let me know it's really over between us I still don't feel the way I used to about Quan. And living with him doesn't feel right anymore either. I have been looking for a condo to move into, and I have an appointment today to look at one. The condo is in an upscale gated community a few minutes from my office so it will be perfect. And once I move out of Quan's house, I can have the girls come over. Quan has no idea I am planning to move out and I am not sure how he is going to take the news.

We have spent the last few days arguing about much of nothing and his attitude toward me has been terrible. He has been acting funny ever since the incident at my parent's house. He acts like I did something wrong, and he brings the situation up consistently. He even told me that if I wouldn't have been conversating with Marquell the altercation wouldn't have happened. But it's not my fault. I didn't add fuel to the fire, he did. But it's easier for Quan to blame me than to take responsibility for his actions. He acts so immature at times.

Fast forward. After much consideration I have decided to move into the condo I looked at. So, soon I will be out of Quan's house and begin the journey of getting back to the best of myself. I realize it's not about Marquell or Quan it's about me. I need to work on myself, I need to build a stronger bond with my girls, and I need to find a good church home. I also need to forgive myself for all I have done and fix my relationship with my parents. My relationship with them is not horrible, but the fact I stayed with Quan after he said what he said to Marquell and upset my Daddy doesn't sit well with them.

After I sign my lease next week, I am going to let Quan know I am moving out. I am not going to tell him yet because that will just give him something else to argue about. But I did let Marquell know, and he was happy to hear that. Marquell told me we will take baby steps with the girls, and I can see them more often once I get all moved out. He said we will start off with one visit for a few hours a week and then overnight visits. I am okay with that, and I will take what I can get. I am sure he just wants to make sure Quan isn't going to be around. But I won't have Quan around the girls. I know that will upset Marquell and the girls too. I am not saying I am not going to be friends with Quan so there may be a chance we hang out or sometimes, but right now I just need some space.

Speaking of Quan, he hasn't come home yet. He has been staying out later and later. I know he likes to go to the bar and have a beer and play pool with the guys, so I assume that's where he is at. I call him but he doesn't answer, so I follow up with a text and still no response. So, I am going to bed. I will see him in the morning.

Morning has come and still no Quan, so I call him again, this time I hear the phone ringing. Quan fell asleep on the couch watching television. I am on my way to the office, so I am not going to bother him. I will just see him later. He has today off and needs the rest.

Today was a good day at the office and when I get back home Quan is awake and in a good mood. I am so glad of that. We have a good conversation, order a pizza, laugh, and have a great night. He told me he will be gone next weekend. He is going to visit his daughter Quantisha who lives almost 600 miles away. They have a great relationship and I love her to pieces. He only gets to see her a couple of times a year since she lives so far, but they talk on the phone and do video calls several times a week. Since Quan will be gone next weekend, I will tell him about my move when he returns. He asked me to go visit Quantisha with him, but London's birthday is next weekend, and I am not missing her birthday party for anything.

Things are cool with Quan and I, but I am still not feeling him in an intimate way. I have outgrown this relationship and I no longer feel attracted to him in a romantic way. He is attractive but I am not attracted to him in sexually. I have heard people say, "they fell out of love." So, I guess the way I feel means I fell out of lust.

Time has flown by, and Quan left this morning to go see his daughter and I am about to get dressed for London's birthday party. I already signed my lease, and I am excited about the move, so I am feeling really good today. I have ordered some furniture and curtains online, and I am ready to lay my condo out. I think I got a little bit of Mama's interior decorating skills.

I need to put on something really cute today for London's birthday party. Looking in my closet I see a curve-fitting blue dress, and this is the perfect dress since it is cute and Marquell's favorite color. It's not too sexy but cute and classy enough for a young girl's birthday party. I am excited to see Marquell and the girls and I am anticipating having a good time with them.

Fast forward. The birthday event is a lot of fun and London is really enjoying herself. I have my back turned to the door, but I hear the girls yell simultaneously "Hi Ms. Angelique!" I look up and see this long-legged exotic looking beauty walking in. I think to myself, who is Ms. Angelique? But it doesn't take me long to see that is Marquell's friend. They are sitting at the table laughing and talking as if I am not even here. And here I sit in this blue dress feeling like a fool. But I need to get my emotions together before how foolish I feel shows on my face. London is about to open her gifts and then I am leaving. As I get up to stand by London so we can sing "Happy Birthday" and she can open her gifts, Marquell gets up and stands by me. I know by the look in my eyes he can tell I am hurt. But I am not going to say anything about his friend being here even though he forbids Quan to be around the girls. It is obvious how Angelique and the girls are interacting that they spend time together.

As I give the girls a hug prior to leaving Marquell feels the need to introduce me to Angelique. But he calls her "Dr. Angelique." Yep, that confirms she is who I think she is, Marquell's friend. He goes on to explain she just wanted to stop by for a few minutes to see London and give her, her birthday gift. As we both walk away from Angelique and toward the door I say, "No need to explain. We are not together anymore, and we are getting ready to get a divorce." But what I am really thinking is if Quan would have come you would have been so mad at me. But I guess that's because of how Quan and I got together. Before I walk out the door Marquell says "Mya, girl you look good in that dress!" I laugh and say, "You better stop before Dr. Angelique hears you." Marquell winks at me and smiles.

I just got back home from the birthday party, and I am glad Quan is not here because he would wonder why I am sitting here at the kitchen table with a pint of ice cream, and mascara running down my face, crying like a baby. I feel so sad right now and it feels like my heart is actually hurting. I literally feel a pain in my chest, not anything medically related, but that pain you feel when you hurt emotionally. So, this is what a broken heart feels like, huh? If you are thinking Mya, you did this to yourself, you are absolutely right. I don't expect any pity because I am reaping what I have sown. I know that, but that doesn't mean it doesn't hurt. I am emotionally crushed. And for some reason, I feel like things will get worse before they get better.

I cried myself to sleep last night and part of me is glad Quan is coming back home today. I can really use a big hug and someone to talk to. But I am making a promise to myself right now that things between us won't go any further. I am not going to end up in a sexual encounter with him.

I need emotional support, not sex. I am not going to tell him why I am feeling the way I am, just that I need some good conversation and a hug.

Quan has made it back home safely and I feel better now. We talked and chilled and I feel back to myself. He is getting tired and said "he feels exhausted" so I am going to tell him tomorrow that I am moving out soon. I am going to take a shower and read for a little bit while he unpacks his last couple of bags. Before getting in the shower, I remember that I need to call my assistant to remind her to bring something to the office in the morning. I could wait but I want to do it now, so I won't forget. As I am getting off the phone, I hear Quan laughing and talking to someone. I lean in toward the door, so I can hear what is going on in the next room. I am just being nosey. I realized Quan is talking to Quantisha on a video call. I think to myself he is such a great dad.

Okay, let me get in the shower so I can relax for the evening. As I begin to move away from the door, I hear Quantisha say "Dad you left your favorite shirt here. I will put it up for you so you can get it whenever you come back to visit us." I think to myself us, what does she mean us? By this time Quantisha's mom is beginning to talk and she is not speaking in a way that makes me believe Quan doesn't deal with her anymore, which is what he told me. As I am listening to this conversation unfold it is evident, they are way more than co-parents. The last straw is when I hear Quantisha's mom say "Quan, don't get yourself in trouble trying to play games. I don't even know why that girl is fooling with you, knowing you ain't no good. That's why you can't be my man. But you can give me more of what you gave me last night any time."

I am in shock at what I am hearing, and it doesn't even seem real. My face feels flushed and I am hurt, disappointed, and angry all at the same time. I can't help but begin to cry. I make my way back into the other room, as Quan hears me coming, he hurries up and ends the video call. I stand directly in front of him. "You done showering already baby?" He asks. "I haven't even gotten in the shower yet," I reply. Standing here staring him down I try to figure out the words to say but instead I slap him as hard as I can and yell "I heard you talking to your baby mama!" He looks stunned. I don't know if he is more stunned by me telling him I heard his conversation or me slapping him.

He tries to give me a hug, I scream "don't you touch me!" I lay on the floor and breakdown. He says, "I am sorry Mya." "Yes, you are, I say. "Sorry and pathetic!" I try to hit him again but this time he grabs my arm and says, "If you want to talk, we can talk but you are not going to keep putting your hands on me." During our heated conversation, he tells me not only has he slept with Quantisha's mom (more than once) but two other women too, including the bartender at the club he goes to, and his co-worker's sister. Then he tries to convince me it's because he always feels like Marquell and I have something going on. Then he says it's because I don't stand up for him when it comes to my family." Now he is saying it's because I didn't divorce Marquell." I have finally had enough of hearing the lies and excuses. I say, "No, you are just a cheating dog, that's why!"

I can't even look at him. I am so furious. I sit on one end of the couch, and he sits on the other end. I am rocking back and forth trying to calm my emotions, but instead, I am getting madder. I can't believe I messed up my marriage for this. I can't believe I fell for the lies again. I can't believe he played me for a fool. I can't believe I lost my marriage, my girls, my home, my reputation, and almost my mind for him, and this is how he repays me. These thoughts are making me feel violent and I am not even a violent person. Marquell told me "Quan brings out the worst in me." And now I see what he means.

The rage has finally consumed me, and I head to the bedroom to get the gun, but as I reach to grab it out of the nightstand, I come to my senses. I am not going to prison for Quan, I have too much to lose, and he is not worth it. Instead of grabbing the gun I grab my lease and throw it at him. "What's this? He asks as he is picking up the papers. I say, "I am moving out. I was going to tell you tomorrow anyway, but this seems like a perfect time." He bites his bottom lip in a nervous way and then says, "we can work this out." I let him know I am not interested in working things out with him. I am going to stay at a hotel for a few days because my condo is almost ready, then I am going to move into my condo, and get my life back on track.

CHAPTER 9

Mending a Broken Marriage

The last two weeks have been hectic I finally got moved into my condo, and I love it. I haven't spoken to Quan, and I have no desire to. The girls spent the night with me a few nights ago and we had a wonderful time. Marquell and I go to divorce court next week, but we are still getting along good. I didn't tell him what happened with Quan because I am too embarrassed. Marquell already knew I was moving out of Quan's house, so he hasn't even asked me anything about him. We don't even talk about Quan.

Marquell is bringing the girls by this evening so I can see them, and I am excited about that. It is such a blessing that we have decided to have a positive friendship for them. Once Lyric's grades begin to drop and she was having trouble at school both Marquell and I became aware of the negative impact our actions were having on the girls. Since we have been getting along better Lyric's grades have improved and both Lyric and London seem happier. They both understand that even though we all don't live together anymore we are still a family. So, our family dynamics are working out. Just because things didn't work out between Marquell and I as a married couple doesn't mean we can't put aside our feelings and do what is best for the girls. That's maturity.

I still love Marquell. I didn't appreciate him when I had him, and I am paying the ultimate price for that. Sometimes we don't realize what we had until it's gone. And we don't know that what we don't want in a person is everything another person is looking for. After the divorce is final, I am sure Marquell will start dating Angelique and that is something I am prepared to deal with. She seems like a nice woman and hasn't done anything to me. Marquell decided not to go out with Angelique or have her around the girls anymore until the divorce is final. He said even though he isn't sleeping with her, it doesn't feel right. He doesn't want people to see him out with her and think he is sleeping with another woman before our divorce is final.

The girls just arrived, and they don't know I finished decorating their bedrooms. When they walk in their rooms, they are ecstatic. I finally feel like I am doing things right and things are looking up for me. I rode by a church earlier today and saw a sign that said, "Don't worry about tomorrow God is already there." That spoke to my heart and gave me peace. I am not perfect, but I have been reading my bible more and praying more. I went to church with Grandma Ronnie recently and that was a turning point for me. The choir sang a song that touched me. And that song helped me to know that God has forgiven me for my actions, now I am on the path to forgiving myself.

Something is happening inside of me. I am not sure what it is, but I feel changed. I feel whole and I feel free. But free in a different way. I don't mean being free from a man but being free from the horrible person I had turned into, being free from turmoil, being free from the cheating and lies, and being free from the stress I had caused myself because of my actions. I fought depression because of my choices, and it was really beginning to get the best of me. But I realized I couldn't redo anything I had done, so I must deal with the results of my decisions and work on being a better me every single day. I found a good therapist and therapy has helped me a lot. I wish I would have gone to a therapist a long time ago. I probably wouldn't be in the situation I am in now. I have learned so much about myself that has helped me to become a better and wiser woman.

Marquell will be coming to pick the girls up soon, I don't want them to leave because I always miss them so much when I am not with them. But they will be back soon for the weekend, so I am making a lot of fun plans. That will be the first time they have a weekend stay with me. I thought it was going to be months before Marquell agreed to let them stay with me for the weekend, but prayer works. I think he sees the authentic change in me. And I believe he knows I am serious about being done with Quan. He may have even had the private investigator follow me around again to make sure I am not still seeing Quan. And if he did, I am not mad about it. Whatever it takes to spend more time with my girls is all right with me. Plus, I don't have anything to hide.

The girls just left, and I am going to spend the free time I have this week decorating. I took some time away from the office to put the finishing touches on my condo. So, I am working from home the rest of the week. Tomorrow I am picking up Mama and we are going to the furniture store so I can buy a couple of throw rugs and pictures. I am looking forward to spending time with her, and she is an expert on decorating.

I wake up to the sun shining and birds chirping, and this feels so good. I haven't felt like this in a long time. Real peace and happiness are priceless. On the way to pick up mama,

I get a call from Daddy asking me to stop by his favorite restaurant and pick up his food order. That's no problem. I am always glad to do things for my parents and they are never an inconvenience. Besides, I have my favorite song playing and I am on an emotional high and stopping at the restaurant will give me more time to enjoy my music.

I pull up to the restaurant and call the phone number on the sign so they can bring Daddy's food order out to me. They said it will be ready in about 5 minutes. I am lost in the moment enjoying the music and ready to conquer the day when I hear a tap on my window. I look up thinking it's Daddy's order, but it's Quan. I look at him and shake my head fast to let him know I am not rolling my car window down to talk to him. I notice his car on the other side of mine, he is here to pick up an order too. About a minute goes by and Quan is still standing there, so I look in my glove compartment and find a pen, then I look in my sun visor and I see a piece of mail I haven't taken into the condo yet. I write on the envelope in all caps, LEAVE ME ALONE!!! I AM DONE!!! And I slam it on the window right in his face. He shakes his head and walks away. And guess what? I don't feel bad for him, and I don't feel any other type of emotions toward him either, like I said I am done with Quan!

I feel so empowered and strong right now. And by the time Daddy's order comes out I am smiling so hard my face feels like it could crack. I back out of the parking spot and speed off bouncing my head up and down to the music not looking Quan's way one time. "Yes, girl!" I yell as loud as I can. I am so proud of myself. When I finally get to my parent's house I am dancing up to the door and feeling amazing. I don't mention a word to my parents about what just happened, this is my moment, not to be shared. This is a private moment between me and God.

This week has been one of the best weeks ever and it's the weekend and the girls are coming over tonight. I went and bought their favorite colors of nail polish, and we are going to cook dinner, make cookies, and have a fingernail painting date. I gave Marquell the code to the gate so he should be ringing the doorbell anytime. After 30 minutes have gone by, I wonder if they are still coming, but before I can call Marquell I hear the doorbell ring. The girls come flying in the door ready for a fun weekend. And that is exactly what it has been, a fun weekend. But it has come to an end. But guess what? Marquell said, they can come back the weekend coming up too. I am so happy to hear that. It's like a dream come true. My girls are my world and when I am with them, I am full of joy, and they are too.

It's a typically busy day at the office today and I received a call from Marquell that I need to return. By the time I call him back he doesn't answer so, I will speak with him later. An hour later he calls me back and we connect. I am eating lunch, so I am in my office and available to talk. He is stopping by the condo later to bring a package to me that for whatever reason was delivered to the house. He said, "it looks important." I told him I can pick up the package from him. But he says, "this evening he will be out close to where I live so it's not an inconvenience." I am glad to hear him say that because I am tired. I just want to go home, kick off these heels, take a hot bath, and relax.

Marquell makes it to the condo about 20 minutes after I get here. He brings in the package and it is something my previous neighbor sent me. She moved out of state and opened a women's clothing store. She sent me a new blazer, hat, and jewelry set she sells at her boutique. It's cute too! There is also a small card included with the package that says "Mya, as soon as I saw this set, I thought of you. It's a gift for how good you have always been to me. Rock this set sis!" That is so sweet of her. I am going to send her a thank you card.

I thank Marquell for bringing the package to me and ask him to give the girls a hug for me when he picks them up from my parents' house. I don't even mention the upcoming divorce I will see him when that date comes. And really there isn't anything to talk about. I yawn unintentionally because I am tired, but Marquell thinks it's a sign that I am ready for him to leave. "No, not at all," I say. That gave him the green light because he got comfortable and sat down and started talking. Before I know it 45 minutes have passed by. But we are having a good time, so I am not going to rush him out the door. I think he needs this time of relaxation too. He works hard and does so much with the girls and for his mom, and I know that can be tiring.

I begin to doze off as Marquell is telling me about something that is going on at his practice. I apologize to him for dozing off and tell him "I need to get ready for bed because I have a long day tomorrow." As he heads toward the door, he stops, turns around, and kisses me on the forehead and then passionately kisses me on the lips, and I am not resisting. I am thinking, what is happening right now? He stops kissing me and takes a deep breath. He holds me tight and says "Mya, I can't stop thinking about you." I don't' know what to say. I was not expecting this. I break away from his hold and start to cry. I am crying because I am happy, I am crying because I feel so bad about how I have treated him, I am crying because I am confused, and I am crying because after all, I have done God is still blessing me. Because this is a blessing.

I can hardly speak as I try to process what is going on. "So, what does this mean Marquell?" "I am not sure," he says. "Let's just enjoy the moment." And that's exactly what we did, and it was magical. I am sure someone was somewhere doing fireworks for the occasion, well, that's how I felt. That intimate moment was unlike anything I have ever experienced with Quan. It was two people deeply in love (not lust), connected on a spiritual level, sharing a bond that can only be described as something God brought together. I never stopped loving Marquell and he never stopped loving me. But now what? Does our intimate experience mean Marquell wants to work on our marriage or was it just a moment that happened that he now regrets? Only time will tell.

I thought maybe since we were intimate Marquell would call me and let me know what the plan for our future is, but I haven't heard from him, and our divorce hearing is in 2 days. We finally completed everything we needed to so that we can move forward. But now I am more confused than ever. I haven't been able to focus on anything because I am upset with myself for allowing what happened with Marquell to happen. I mean Marquell is still my husband so it's not a bad thing, I just feel bad. I am beginning to feel like he just wanted to sleep with me one more time before the divorce. Now, I feel like he was saying all the things he said to me to make me feel like there is something still between us. I guess I deserve this too. But I will bounce back from this as well. I am going to walk into the courtroom with my head up and not even let Marquell know how hurt I am.

Well, today is our court date and I feel sick at the stomach. It's just my nerves. I am going to be a single woman after today and this chapter of my life will officially come to an end. But I am not going to give up on myself or give up on finding someone to truly love me again. I learned my lesson and I will never commit adultery again; I will never let another man tempt me away from what God has blessed me with, and I will never take for a good man for granted.

I am driving as slow as I can to the courthouse. I am dreading going and not in a rush to get there. I want to turn around and go back home. Deep inside, I don't want this divorce to happen. Maybe I should just not go to the divorce hearing, but if I don't show up, I might get arrested or something. So, I better show up. Plus, I don't have the right to not show to court and prolong things for Marquell. He deserves the happy life I couldn't give him.

As I walk in the courtroom, I see Marquell, our attorneys and the judge. I say a quick prayer and ask God to help me stay calm because I feel like I can have an emotional breakdown at any minute. As the hearing begins Marquell's attorney asks the judge if he can speak to him. He walks up to the judge's bench to speak with the judge, and I am trying to figure out what he is saying. But the judge has put his hand over the microphone so I can't make out what they are discussing.

I am beginning to feel anxious now because I think Marquell is going to try to get full custody of the girls. Is that why he slept with me? Did he set me up so that I would be blindsided with this? "Lord, please don't let him take the girls from me." I feel the tears beginning to roll down my face. At the same time, the judge calls Marquell's name. I think, here we go. It's time. "Yes sir," Marquell responds. The judge proceeds to speak "It is my understanding you no longer want a divorce. Is that right?" I look at Marquell and my face is soak and wet now. I can't believe what I am hearing. "That's correct," Marquell says. My attorney looks as if she doesn't know whether to look shocked or smile, it's a mix of both.

I run across the room and hold Marquell as tight as I can. I say, "thank you for giving me another chance." He smiles and says, "God gave you another chance." He went on to explain that he has been praying for us and wanted to make sure he heard from God correctly and that he wasn't acting out of emotions. He wanted to make sure the love was still there, and that he didn't sleep with me out of emotions or want to get back with me out of emotions. He said the moment he kissed me at the condo the real love emerged from underneath all we have been through. I feel so grateful right now, so grateful that I can't even put it into words. I look up and say "God, thank you...thank you... thank you!!" Now I know how Cinderella felt when she got her glass slippers.

As we continue to move forward things are better than ever. Marquell has forgiven me, and I have forgiven myself. I have not stopped praying for my marriage and neither has he. The girls were so happy when they found out we were not getting a divorce. My family was bubbling up with joy when I told them what happened in court. Angelique took the news well and surprisingly so did Chris and Marquell's mom. They all see I am different, and they all said, "whatever makes Marquell happy makes them happy."

The journey I have been on has deepened my faith and has helped me to learn about redemption. I never told Marquell about finding out Quan was cheating. And I didn't have to because Marquell shared with me that while I was living with Quan, he was praying that God would reveal to me the kind of man he really is. Because Marquell said, "any man that would intentionally try to break up another man's home is not a good man." Wow, he was right.

If you are wondering if I will ever cheat on my husband again, I can assure you I never will. Almost losing my family for good devastated me. I did something stupid without thinking about the consequences. I made choices that hurt the ones I love the most, and I must live with that for the rest of my life.

Marquell and I are starting a new beginning and our ending will be perfect. We will grow old together and always be thankful for how God mended our broken marriage. To celebrate getting back together Marquell asked if we can have a recommitment ceremony. I said "yes," and I know it is going to be the start of something more beautiful and more blessed than either one of us can imagine.

CHAPTER 10

The Recommitment Ceremony

Today is our recommitment ceremony. We are sharing our special moment with some of our closest family and friends. We are not having anything too big or too fancy, just a small ceremony, dinner, and dancing. The event will be starting in an hour, and I am looking forward to it. The event center is decorated so beautifully, and I know everything will be perfect. I am wearing a royal blue and silver short but classy dress, with silver jewelry, and royal blue and silver heels. I have my hair pinned up in a glamorous bun. Marquell has a royal blue suit on with a silver bow tie, and a pair of royal blue shoes. We already did a big wedding so this time we want it to feel like a party, a celebration.

The time is winding down and the ceremony will begin soon. I can see through the curtains in the room I am in, and the parking lot is near full. I am very excited, but I don't know who is more excited me or Ebony. She loves me so much and she loves Marquell and she is happy that we got back together. She has always believed in us and knowing she was praying for us meant the world to both of us.

The ceremony is now beginning, and I see all the smiling faces as I enter the room the ceremony is being held in. The minister does his part and Marquell and I say the words we wrote for each other. Nothing is mentioned about why we were apart only that we are now back together and how wonderful the rest of our life is going to be. The girls are grinning so big you would think they are on a vacation at their favorite amusement park. I look at their smiles and feel like I won the lottery. This feeling is absolutely priceless.

The ballroom where dinner is being served is gorgeous. The flowers, the lights, the decorations, just beautiful. I can't wait to finish eating so we can dance and have fun. Both Marquell and I like to dance, and he is a great dancer. I let the DJ know that shortly he needs to switch from the soft jazz music to some dancing music because it's almost time to party.

This food is delicious and cooked to perfection. I wasn't sure what to choose for dinner, so we opted for a buffet with lots of different choices. If you could see the way I have the roast beef, potatoes, green beans, meatloaf, corn, shrimp, and meatballs stacked on my plate, you might think I haven't eaten for days. And it's not even time for cake yet.

Before I can finish my plate of food, I hear the party music begin to play. I grab Marquell and we move toward the dance floor, and we are dancing so hard we both are sweating. If I don't slow down my bun is going to fall down, because I see a couple of bobby pins on the floor. This really is a celebration, and we have a lot to celebrate, so if all my bobby pins end up on the floor I don't care. I have family here that are beauticians, and they can hook my hair right back up.

Hours have now gone by and it's time to wrap this night up. Marquell and I have a romantic getaway planned for the next few days, and we are leaving early in the morning. We are going to a beautiful resort. We wanted to go there years ago but never got around to it, but we are not missing out on the opportunity this time. When we return from our trip I am officially moving back home. We have been staying at the house and the condo since we got back together, but now it's time for me to let the condo go and go back to my home, not just to my house, but to my home.

It's still surreal to me that Marquell and I are back together. I woke up the other morning thinking it was a dream. But I rolled over in the bed and there was Marquell right next to me, I smiled and thanked God again because what I have dreamed about happening so many times is now my reality. My marriage is stronger than it has ever been. Before the affair, we talked about God being in our marriage, but we didn't have him in it the way we needed to. But now we understand why having God as the glue to our marriage is so important. I know without God our marriage would not have been repaired. This is something we couldn't have accomplished on our own. I remember when I would always say "I would never cheat on my husband." I would hear about other women who were cheating on their husbands, and I would call them all kinds of names. But anything can happen if you don't keep God first in your marriage. I learned that the hard way. I know the difference between keeping God first in your marriage, and not keeping God first in your marriage, and keeping him first in your marriage makes all the difference.

In a marriage you have good times and bad times, you have ups and downs, and you have struggles and successes. But the key is to go through it all having God on your team. Marquell and I used to pray together when we were dating and when we first got married but then we got "too busy," and things changed. But now we realize we can't allow that to happen. We are committed to doing whatever we need to do to have the best marriage possible. We even have a marriage success wall in our bedroom. The wall has family pictures, marriage scriptures, positive affirmations about marriage, and our marriage goals for the next twelve months. And we look at it every single day. We take time out to do the small things that can lead to big changes in our marriage today, tomorrow, and in the days to come. Our marriage is for a lifetime, and every single day for the rest of my life I will show my husband how much I love and appreciate him.

Conclusion

Five years have passed since Marquell and I got back together. There is not a day that goes by that I don't thank God for giving me and my marriage another chance. I got my phone number changed and blocked Quan on social media. That is what my new start included, totally letting go of the past. Marquell didn't ask me to change my phone number or to block Quan on social media, those are things I wanted to do. Quan hasn't bothered me or anything like that, I just wanted to shut off all ways he could contact me because we have no reason to communicate.

The girls are doing great and are growing up fast. Marquell and I are back active in our community as a couple. We recently hosted a charity event, and we lead marriage seminars and conferences. We both received certifications as marriage retreat leaders, and we have been blessed to help heal many marriages. Our retreats usually sell out and we receive a lot of positive feedback from the couples that attend them.

At first, I was embarrassed to share our story with other people who didn't know us but being transparent has been a necessity when helping others. And eventually, the feeling of embarrassment went away. People really like the fact that I am open and honest about what Marquell and I went through.

We consistently do things to improve our marriage whether that means a weekend escape, date night, shutting off our cells phone and talking, or taking time away from work to simply enjoy family time. We also created "bring it to the table" where we talk about any issues that are bothering us, whether big or small. We also recently finished an advanced communication and trust class. We are constantly learning about the important elements of a successful marriage.

I believe faith and prayer work. I ended up right where I am supposed to be, with who I am supposed to be with. Thank you, Lord, for forgiveness, for my family, and for my future. Love, Mya.

About the Author

Dr. Shauntel Peak-Jimenez, Ph.D., is an author, life and success coach, coach trainer, business owner, and woman of faith. She is passionate about inspiring others through writing, speaking, and teaching programs.

Many years ago, she was a teen mother and single mother of five living on welfare. Through faith and determination, she overcame many obstacles. She is grateful to God and her family and friends for helping her become who she is today.

Made in the USA
Las Vegas, NV
20 December 2021

38944932R00052